# GUS & GERTIE

## AND
# THE LUCKY CHARMS

by JOAN LOWERY NIXON

pictures by DIANE deGROAT

SEASTAR BOOKS

New York

Text © 2001 by Joan Lowery Nixon
Illustrations © 2001 by Diane deGroat
First SeaStar Books paperback edition published in 2002.

SeaStar Books
A division of North-South Books Inc.

First published in the United States by SeaStar Books, a division of North-South Books Inc., New York.
Published simultaneously in Great Britain, Canada, Australia, and New Zealand by North-South Books,
an imprint of Nord-Süd Verlag AG, Gossau Zürich, Switzerland.

Library of Congress Cataloging-in-Publication Data.
Nixon, Joan Lowery.
Gus & Gertie and the lucky charms / by Joan Lowery Nixon; pictures by Diane deGroat.
p.   cm.
Summary: Penguins Gus and Gertie take part in the Animals Winter Olympics.
[1. Olympics—Fiction. 2. Penguins—Fiction. 3. Animals—Fiction.] I. Title: Gus and Gertie and the lucky charms.
II. De Groat, Diane, ill. III. Title.
PZ7.N65 Gt 2002
[Fic]—dc21    2001034405
A CIP catalogue record for this book is available from The British Library.

The art for this book was prepared using watercolor.
The text for this book is set in 16-point Nueva MM.

ISBN 1-58717-099-X (trade edition)
HC 10 9 8 7 6 5 4 3 2 1
ISBN 1-58717-100-7 (library edition)
LE 10 9 8 7 6 5 4 3 2 1
ISBN 1-58717-158-9 (paperback edition)
PB 10 9 8 7 6 5 4 3 2 1

Printed in Singapore
For more information about our books, and the authors and artists who create them, visit our web site: www.northsouth.com

With love to my grandson,
Timothy William Quinlan
—J. L. N.

# CHAPTER 1

Gus and Gertie looked down at the ice skaters on the lake. Then they looked above at the skiers on the hill. Finally, they stared in awe at the banner stretched over a big white tent. WELCOME TO THE ANIMALS' WINTER OLYMPIC GAMES, it read.

Gertie bounced with glee, and the rubber flowers on her swim cap fluttered. "Just think, Gus!" she said. "We're the very first to come from Antarctica to take part in these games."

Gus glanced at Gertie's swim cap and sighed. "Do we have to wear flowered swim caps?" he asked.

"We are synchronized swimmers," Gertie said. "You know very well that synchronized swimmers always wear matching caps and swim together with beautiful strokes." She patted the shiny goldfish pin on her scarf. "Who knows? With my lucky charm, we might even win a medal."

A gangly goose who was leaving the tent said to Gertie, "You have a lucky charm? *I* had a lucky charm, but it disappeared."

"What happened?" Gertie asked.

"I don't know, but take my advice," the goose muttered. "Take care of your lucky charm. It's crowded inside the tent, and I think someone in there is up to no good."

As the gangly goose waddled down the hill, Gus said, "I don't want to meet anyone who is up to no good. Why don't we go home?"

"And miss our chance to be in the Olympics?" Gertie answered. "No. We're staying. And while we're here, Gus, be sure to take lots and lots of Polaroid pictures."

"Pictures of what?" Gus asked. "Nobody's doing anything but going in and out of that big tent."

"Those are not nobodies," Gertie told him. "Those are famous athletes." As a group swept by, Gertie spied a splendid swan. She gasped.

"I've seen you on television!" she cried to the swan. "You're a famous ice skater. May I have your autograph? Gus, take our picture!"

The swan smiled sweetly and scribbled her signature on a slip of paper.

Gertie eyed the gold four-leaf clover the swan wore on a chain around her neck. "Is that your lucky charm?" she asked.

"Yes," the swan said. "I wear it every time I skate."

A furry fox winked at Gertie and held up a key chain. A shiny copper penny dangled at one end. "Just take a look at this," he said. "My genuine lucky penny is the best lucky charm there is. It's going to bring me a win in the speed skating."

"That's what you think," a wiggly wallaby shouted. "*I'm* going to win. Take a look at my lucky four-leaf clover set in silver."

A small voice piped up near Gertie. "They haven't got a chance because I'm not only a better skater, I've got a lucky rabbit's foot." A raggedy rabbit struggling to keep up with the crowd pointed at his own foot. "I take my lucky foot everywhere I go."

Gertie looked around. She could see lots of sparkling lucky charms throughout the crowd. She whispered to Gus, "Everyone may have a lucky charm, but everyone can't win. So who will the winners be?"

"The ones who train the most and work the hardest and—"

Gus couldn't finish because at that moment a bobsled team of big brown bears rushed up to them. Gertie and Gus were swept inside the tent.

# CHAPTER
# 2

Gus and Gertie suddenly found themselves caught in a hubbub of gaggling geese, furry foxes, overwrought otters, rowdy roadrunners, bumbling bears, and downright daffy dingoes. Some were hurrying. Some were scurrying. Some were standing in line. And back and forth throughout the tent scampered happy helpers in snappy red-and-white uniforms with OFFICIAL printed on their caps.

"This way! That way! Get in line!" A mannerly mouse in an official uniform waved a sign that said ANY QUESTIONS? ASK ME.

Gus took his picture.

"I have a question," Gertie told the mouse. "A goose told us that someone in this tent is up to no good. Do you know who that someone is?"

The mouse shrugged. "Don't ask me," he said.

"But your sign says to ask you," Gertie told him.

"Only if I have the answers," the mouse said.

Two happy helpers with waggily whis-
kers ran over Gertie's feet. "Ooops! Sorry, luv,"
one of them said. "We're busy, busy, busy."

Before the happy helpers disappeared
into the crowd, Gus took pictures of them.

"Never mind those two," Gertie told Gus. "They aren't really sorry. They're bumping into nearly everyone in the tent."

Gus sighed. "Are you sure you want to be in the Winter Olympics, Gertie? If we stayed home, we could relax and watch all the events on television."

"I want to be in the Olympics," Gertie insisted. "It will be a dream come true."

Four daffy dingoes leaped past. One did a back flip, nearly landing on Gertie. "G'day,

g'day," he said. "Wait till you see me do that on skis! What a fine sight I'll be."

A beefy badger bumped into line behind Gertie and Gus. "Skiing is not as exciting as bobsledding," he said. "Speeding down a snow-packed trail—now that's a real sport."

"Ha! Racing on skates is even better," the raggedy rabbit said.

Gertie smiled to herself. She knew that synchronized swimming was the best sport of all.

Finally Gus and Gertie reached the table where a harried hedgehog sat. He frowned from under his OFFICIAL hat and yelled, "Next!"

The mouse ran up to the table leg and smiled at Gertie. "Do you have any other questions? I have lots of answers I haven't used yet."

The harried hedgehog scowled. "What are you doing here?" he asked. "You're a mouse. You're supposed to be working on the computer. NEXT!" he yelled again.

"That's us," Gertie said.

"We came to register for an Olympic event," Gus told the hedgehog.

"Synchronized swimming," Gertie added proudly. She pointed to her swim cap. "See? I'm wearing part of my costume."

The hedgehog sighed with impatience. "Swimming events are in the Summer Olympics, when it's warm, not in the Winter Olympics, when it's cold. No one can swim in ice water."

Gus and Gertie stared at each other in surprise. "Where *we* come from," Gertie said, "*everyone* swims in ice water."

"It doesn't matter!" The harried hedgehog pulled out a large official stamp. But since he had no papers to stamp, he stamped the table with a loud *thump*.

"Positively no swimming in the Winter Olympics!" he shouted so loudly that everyone in the tent heard him. "You can either apply to enter another event or you can sit and watch."

"Oh, dear. What shall we do?" Gertie asked Gus.

Gus didn't have a chance to answer because at that moment someone screamed.

# CHAPTER 3

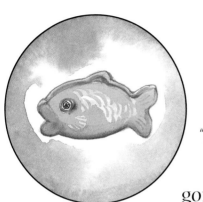

"My lucky charm is missing!" the swan sobbed. "Someone has taken it!"

"My lucky penny has gone missing!" the fox fumed.

"My lucky four-leaf clover has been stolen!" the wallaby whined.

"My lucky charm's gone, too!" someone else cried.

"And mine!"

"And mine!"

Alarmed, Gertie reached up to make sure her lucky goldfish pin was in place.

It wasn't.

"Oh, Gus!" Gertie cried. "My lucky charm is missing, too! Call the police!"

The hubbub in the tent grew louder.

The hedgehog pounded on the table. "Everyone quiet down!" he shouted. "I'm in charge here."

As soon as they were all silent, the hedgehog said, "What's all this silly fuss about lucky charms? No one wins because of lucky charms. They win because of skill and hard work."

"But I like my lucky charm," the swan said. "I want it back."

"And I want my lucky charm," the fox insisted.

"I want mine, too!" others cried.

Suddenly Gertie got an idea. "I know when my charm must have been stolen," she said. "It was when someone bumped into me."

"Of course!" the swan said. "The thief must have been a bear! The big brown bears bumped into everyone!"

"I think the thief was a dingo," the wallaby said. "The daffy dingoes bumped into me."

"It's crowded in here," the fox yelled. "We were all getting bumped."

"Quiet!" the hedgehog called out. He pounded the table again. Then he asked, "Who saw the thief? What did he look like?"

The swan raised a wing. "If he was a bear, he was tall and wide."

"If he was a dingo," the wallaby said, "he was short and thin."

Others spoke up. "I think the thief wore a dark blue sweater."

"No. He wore a green-and-yellow jacket."

"His hat was over his eyes."

"He didn't have a hat."

"I have something to say," Gus told the hedgehog. He studied his photos as he placed them on the hedgehog's desk.

But the hedgehog didn't listen to Gus. Instead, he turned to the mouse. "Type the descriptions of the thief into the computer," he ordered. "Print a copy, and then all the witnesses can sign it."

"I have something *important* to say," Gus said.

Again the hedgehog didn't listen. "We must do everything we can to find the thief who stole the lucky charms," he announced.

"Then listen to Gus!" Gertie shouted.

The hedgehog's quills quivered with indignation. "*I'm* the official. *I'm* in charge, not you," he snapped at Gus.

"Take a look at these photographs," Gus said. "If you study them, you will find two important clues that will help us find the thief."

The hedgehog looked over Gus's left shoulder and frowned. "What clues?" he asked.

The mouse climbed to Gertie's shoulder to get a better look. "Are there any pictures of me?" he asked.

Gertie looked over Gus's right shoulder. "You took too many pictures of those whiskery happy helpers," she said.

"Take a good look at the helpers," Gus told her. "What do you see?"

Gertie took a closer look. "Two of them are wearing uniforms, but look how they misspelled OFISHUL on their caps. They aren't happy helpers. They don't belong here."

Gus said to the hedgehog, "Gertie is right. And see—wherever they've been, lucky charms have disappeared."

"I know who they are," the mouse said. "Their names are Mugs and Thugs."

The hedgehog squinted at the photographs. "One of the thieves is holding a small leather bag. Is that a bit of gold chain I see dangling from the bag?"

"Yes," Gus said. "And that's the second clue."

"Those must be our lucky charms!" the swan cried. "Arrest Mugs and Thugs right this minute!"

"But where are they?" the badger asked.

Gertie looked up to see Mugs and Thugs edging out of the tent. "There they go!" she shouted. "After them, Gus! We can't let them get away!"

# CHAPTER 4

As everyone ran away from the tent, Gertie pointed to the ski lift. Mugs and Thugs were riding up the side of the mountain.

"There they are!" Gertie cried.

She and Gus hopped onto a seat behind them.

The mouse jumped on with them. So did the wallaby, the badger, and the rabbit. The seat swung back and forth, rising slowly.

"Mugs and Thugs will stay ahead of us. We'll never catch them this way," Gertie complained.

"Wait until we reach the top of the mountain," Gus told her.

"But they'll reach it first," the mouse said.

"Before we get there," the wallaby said.

Gertie gasped as she saw Mugs and Thugs leap from the ski lift at the top of the mountain.

"They're headed for the ski runs," the rabbit said.

"Look! They're stopping to put on skis," the mouse said.

As Gus and Gertie reached the top, Gus held Gertie's flipper. They jumped off the lift together.

"Mugs and Thugs have started down the mountain!" the rabbit cried.

"We're too late!" the wallaby groaned.

"We don't have skis," the badger said.

"Gus and I don't need skis," Gertie told him as they ran toward the ski jump. "We're made for sliding."

Gus and Gertie pushed off from the top of the ski jump. They slid down on their bellies so fast that at the end of the ramp they sailed off high into the air. As they came down, they landed right on top of the escaping thieves.

"Get off!" Mugs yelled at Gus as they continued down the mountainside.

Thugs shouted at Gertie, "Your flippers are over my eyes! I can't see where I'm going!"

"Give back the lucky charms you stole," Gertie demanded. She tried to reach for the bag Mugs was holding.

"We took 'em fair and square," Mugs said. "We're pack rats. Taking bright and shiny things is what pack rats do."

"That doesn't mean it's right," Gus said. He grabbed for the bag of lucky charms.

"Gus! Watch out!" Gertie screeched. "We're off the ski run!"

"Help! We're headed for the bobsleds!" Thugs shouted.

"Stop! Stop!" Gertie cried.

But they were skiing too fast to stop. The four of them landed on an empty bobsled. It shot off down the icy bobsled trail.

"Let go! You're choking me!" shouted Thugs.

The bobsled suddenly shot around a curve and sailed up over the side. Through the air and over the heads of the crowd it flew.

"We're going to crash in the lake!" Mugs screamed.

"Help! We can't swim!" Thugs cried.

The bobsled came down hard. It smacked into the thin ice on the lake, and through the ice it plunged, sinking deep into the cold water.

# CHAPTER 5

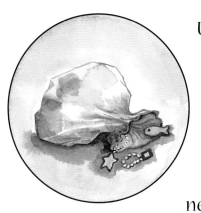

Up through the water Gus swam. He held the bag of lucky charms in one flipper and Mugs in the other. Gertie swam next to Gus. She gripped Thugs tightly.

Together they burst up through the hole in the ice. They pushed Mugs and Thugs to safety and tossed the bag of lucky charms to shore. Then they did two twirls, a flip, and a triple leap in and out of the water to celebrate.

The crowd at the lake cheered and clapped loudly.

"Gus and Gertie broke the ski jump distance record," the mouse announced.

"Disqualified!" the hedgehog shouted. He straightened his official hat as he hurried to the front of the crowd. "They weren't wearing skis."

"They broke the bobsled speed record, too," the mouse insisted.

"Disqualified!" the hedgehog snapped. "They broke the bobsled."

The mouse drew himself up as tall as he could. "Their synchronized swimming was the very best ever," he said.

"Disqualified!" the hedgehog growled. "I already told you, no swimming events in the Winter Olympics. That's my official ruling."

Gertie shrugged. "I don't mind being officially disqualified," she told the mouse. "Because Gus and I *feel* like winners." She laughed and said to Gus, "You were right. We didn't need a single lucky charm to do it!"

Gus patted Gertie's shoulder. "Now that we've taken part in the Olympic Games, why don't we just go back to Antarctica and watch the rest on television?"

The hedgehog shook his head so hard that he almost lost his official hat. "You *haven't* taken part in the Animals' Winter Olympic Games. They haven't officially begun. And they won't until the parade tomorrow when I blow my official whistle!"

The mouse sighed. "I'm sorry, Gertie," he said. "The Olympic Games always begin with a parade. Athletes from each country march in it."

"Alphabetically," the hedgehog said.

Gertie smiled at the mouse. "Do you remember what countries are at the front of the line?"

The mouse thought for a moment. "Afghanistan, Albania, Algeria, Angola . . . But none of them sent athletes this time." Suddenly he jumped up and down with excitement. "That means Antarctica is first on the list! Gus and Gertie from Antarctica can lead the parade!"

Gertie's smile grew even wider. "Thank you. We'd be delighted," she said.

The crowd cheered again, but the hedgehog waved for quiet. "Wait!" he said. "I have to think!"

He grumbled to himself as he straightened his official hat. Then he mumbled to himself as he smoothed his official tie.

Finally, the hedgehog looked up. "Antarctica is *not* an official country. It's just a piece

of land," he told the crowd. "But this is my very own official ruling. Gus and Gertie from Antarctica may lead the parade *and* carry the Olympic Games' flag." He scowled at the mouse. "I officially thought that last part up—not you."

"Oh, thank you!" Gertie said. She hugged Gus. Then she hugged the mouse. "Leading the parade will be the most wonderful part of the Animals' Winter Olympic Games!"

And it was.